Sports Illustrated
KIDS

FOOTBALL'S
ORIGIN STORY

by Robb Murray

CAPSTONE PRESS
a capstone imprint

Published by Capstone Press, an imprint of Capstone
1710 Roe Crest Drive, North Mankato, Minnesota 56003
capstonepub.com

Library of Congress Cataloging-in-Publication Data
Names: Murray, Robb, author.
Title: Football's origin story / by Robb Murray.
Description: North Mankato, Minnesota : Capstone Press, [2025] | Series: Sports
illustrated kids: sports origin stories | Includes bibliographical references and index.
| Audience: Ages 8-11 | Audience: Grades 4-6 | Summary: "A last-second pass!
A scramble to the end zone. You love the adrenaline of football. But where and
how did this rough-and-tumble sport begin? What were the original rules? What
equipment did players use? And how has the sport changed since then? Get the
answers to all your questions and more!"— Provided by publisher.
Identifiers: LCCN 2024022743 (print) | LCCN 2024022744 (ebook) |
ISBN 9781669090403 (hardcover) | ISBN 9781669090359 (paperback) |
ISBN 9781669090366 (pdf) | ISBN 9781669090380 (kindle edition) |
ISBN 9781669090373 (epub)
Subjects: LCSH: Football—History—Juvenile literature.
Classification: LCC GV950.7 .M865 2025 (print) | LCC GV950.7 (ebook) |
DDC 796.332/2—dc23/eng/20240520
LC record available at https://lccn.loc.gov/2024022743
LC ebook record available at https://lccn.loc.gov/2024022744

Editorial Credits
Editor: Mandy Robbins; Designer: Elyse White; Media Researcher: Jo Miller;
Production Specialist: Tori Abraham

Image Credits
AP Images, 21; Getty Images: Bettmann, 11, 24, Bob Thomas/Popperfoto, 10, David
Madison, cover (top), Gregory Shamus, 9, Hulton Archive, 8, 23, Mike Ehrmann,
5, Patrick Smith, 13; Ryan Kang via AP, 28; Shutterstock: Eric Glenn, 15; Sports
Illustrated: Bob Rosato, 27, Erick W. Rasco, 17, 26, John Biever, 20, Neil Leifer,
18, Peter Read Miller, 19; Superstock: Everett Collection, 12, H. ARMSTRONG
ROBERTS/ClassicStock, 14, Underwood Photo Archives, 6; Wikimedia: University
of Washington/Museum of History and Industry, cover (bottom)

Printed and bound in China. 6098

TABLE OF CONTENTS

Words in **bold** are in the glossary.

THE GREATEST SUPER BOWL COMEBACK

It was February 5, 2017—Super Bowl LI. The greatest quarterback of all time looked defeated. Tom Brady's New England Patriots were down 28–3, late in the third quarter. It would take a miracle for the Patriots to come back and win.

For most quarterbacks, this would be a problem. But Tom Brady wasn't most quarterbacks, and this game was far from over. Brady and the Patriots charged back to win 34–28 in overtime. It was the biggest comeback in Super Bowl history!

Tom Brady throws a pass during Super Bowl LI.

In the stands, more than 70,000 people watched the dramatic comeback. More than 111 million people around the world watched it on TV.

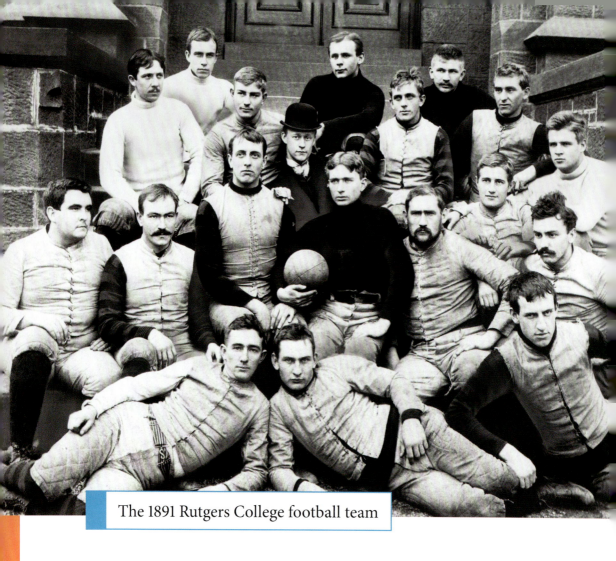

The 1891 Rutgers College football team

All of this is a far cry from the sport's humble beginnings. The first football game took place in 1869. Back then, TV didn't exist. The only people watching were the friends and classmates of the college players.

When the game was invented, women and people of color weren't allowed to play. Today, football has become a diverse sport including women's professional football leagues. Nearly everything about football has changed since that first game. And its popularity continues to grow.

THE FIRST GAME

The first football game took place in New Jersey between Rutgers University and Princeton University. A few years earlier, Princeton crushed Rutgers 40–2 in baseball. Then, in 1869, the Rutgers crew decided to invite the Princeton boys over to play a new game called football. Rutgers won 6–4.

CHAPTER 1
CHANGING A ROUGH SPORT

The official rules of football were first written down by Walter Camp in 1876. He is known as the "father of American football." Touchdowns were worth five points. Field goals were worth four. Years later, those rules were changed to make touchdowns worth six points and field goals worth three.

Walter Camp, 1870s

Michigan Stadium, also called "The Big House"

Stadiums and playing surfaces have changed completely too. In the early days, games were played on grass on college campuses. Today professional games take place in huge stadiums, about half of which use **artificial turf**. The nation's largest stadium is at the University of Michigan. It's called "The Big House." It can hold 107,601 fans.

Football equipment has changed a lot since the sport began. The first football players wore no safety equipment at all! The effects could be terrible. Between 1890 and 1905, 45 young men were killed playing college football, the most popular level of the game at the time. In 1905, President Theodore Roosevelt urged coaches to make the game safer. They did this in two ways. First, they introduced the forward pass. They also changed the rules to stop the game when a ball carrier was down.

THE FORWARD PASS

In the rough early years, football plays started with players huddling together in an often dangerous, rough-and-tumble **scrum**. After dozens of players died, changes were made to make the game safer. The most important change came in 1905 with the introduction of the forward pass. Passing spread players out, opening up the game to more action.

1938 Heisman-Trophy winner
Davey O'Brien throws a pass.

Teams began using leather helmets during the
1920s. They weren't much compared to today's highly
padded hard plastic shells, but it was a start. By the
1950s, helmets had **face masks**. Today's helmets are
designed to help prevent major head wounds as well
as **concussions**.

Notre Dame University football players model the 1880s padding on the left and "updated" 1930s padding on the right.

Shoulder pads had come along even before helmets. Princeton University's L. P. Smock fashioned the first known set of shoulder pads in 1877. By the 1960s most professional players wore the kind of heavy-duty shoulder pads seen today.

At first, players wore whatever shoes they had. The first cleats came along in 1920. Cleats were meant to help players grip the ground when running. They consisted of metal claw-like pieces screwed into pre-drilled holes in the soles of the shoes. Today, cleat designs by brands such as Nike and Adidas not only protect feet but also enhance performance.

Nike cleats worn by Philadelphia Eagles quarterback Carson Wentz in 2019

FACT

Today, more people in the United States watch and follow football than any other sport.

CHAPTER 2
LEAGUES, MERGERS, AND CHAMPIONSHIPS

The National Football League (NFL) was established in 1920 in Canton, Ohio. There were 14 teams when the league launched. In 1960, the American Football League (AFL) played its first season. The two leagues competed for players and fans for years. They finally came together in 1966.

In 1950, the AFL's Cleveland Browns defeated the NFL's Philadelphia Eagles.

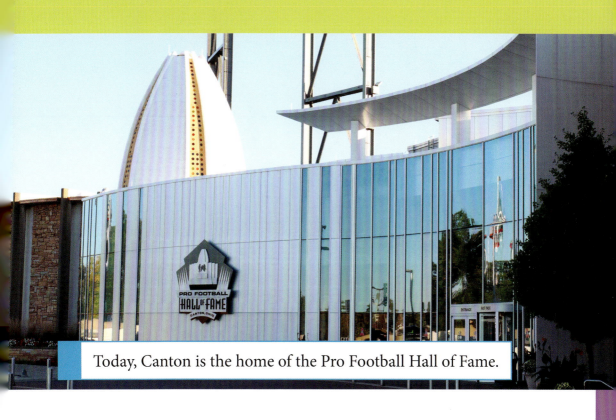
Today, Canton is the home of the Pro Football Hall of Fame.

But the NFL isn't the only game in town. Today, momentum is building for several women's football leagues. The Women's Football Alliance (WFA) is a professional, full-contact football league. Established in 2009, about 60 teams compete in three divisions. The top division is called WFA Pro.

Today, the "big game" that matters most is the Super Bowl. It was first called the AFL-NFL World Championship Game. The league changed the game's name to the Super Bowl in 1969. The first Super Bowl saw the Green Bay Packers defeat the Kansas City Chiefs 35–10.

CHAPTER 3
LEADERS IN THE SPORT

The most successful teams in NFL history are the New England Patriots and the Pittsburgh Steelers. Both have won six Super Bowl titles. The San Francisco 49ers and Dallas Cowboys are right behind them with five apiece. The Green Bay Packers and New York Giants each have won four. The team with the most regular season wins, however, is the Green Bay Packers. The Chicago Bears have only one Super Bowl win to their name, but they are right behind the Packers in overall wins.

FACT

The Arizona Cardinals have the most losses in NFL history. Through the 2023 season, they recorded a whopping 803 losses.

Patriots wide receiver Julian Edelmen is interviewed after winning the 2019 Super Bowl.

Teams are made up of players, but they're not the only people on the field. Officials, coaches, and announcers have also been leaders on the football field.

The NFL is full of star players, but some shine brighter than the rest. The greatest quarterback of all time is probably Tom Brady. Brady holds the career passing yards record with 89,214. But the record for the most passing yards in a game was set way back in 1951. No one has topped Norm Van Brocklin's 554 yards.

Norm Van Brocklin in action in a 1960 game

FACT

The record for most passing yards in a single season is held by Peyton Manning. He threw for 5,477 yards in 2013.

The NFL's all-time leading **rusher** is Emmitt Smith. He ran for 18,355 yards over a 15-year career. The record for most yards in one season belongs to Eric Dickerson, who ran for 2,105 yards in 1984.

The middle linebacker is one of the most important players on defense. In that position, Ray Lewis holds the title. No other middle linebacker has both 41.5 **sacks** and 31 **interceptions**.

Emmitt Smith, 2002

Successful teams have good coaches, and few coaches could top Bill Belichick. He led the Patriots to six Super Bowl wins and has the third-most victories in NFL history. Vince Lombardi is close behind. He led the Green Bay Packers to five NFL titles and was known as a master motivator.

Winning isn't the only way a coach can affect the game. When Howard "Red" Hickey coached the San Francisco 49ers from 1959 to 1963, he used a new way to start a play—the shotgun formation. It was named for the way it spreads receivers all over the field.

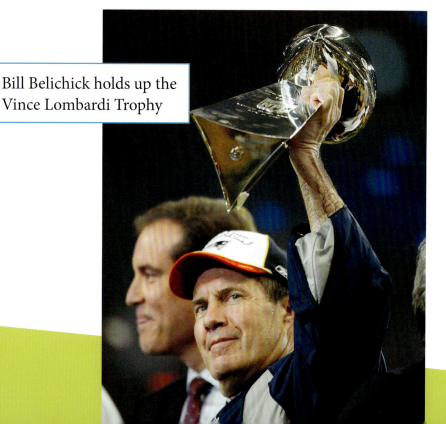

Bill Belichick holds up the Vince Lombardi Trophy

The Dallas Cowboys running the shotgun formation

That wasn't the only new idea to come to the NFL out of San Francisco. Bill Walsh took over the 49ers in 1979. Years earlier, as an assistant coach with the Cincinnati Bengals, he devised a new style of offense. It used mostly pass plays, often for short yardage, as a way of controlling the ball. It became known as the West Coast Offense.

FACT

During the 1972–73 season, Don Shula coached the Miami Dolphins to a perfect, undefeated season, including a Super Bowl win. No other team has ever done this!

There was a time when **racism** limited access to professional football to white men. Eventually, pioneering players pushed through barriers to change that. Their determination and leadership have made the sport accessible to all ethnicities.

Ignacio "Lou" Molinet was the first Hispanic player in the NFL. He played one season for the Frankford Yellow Jackets in 1927, helping the team to a seventh-place finish.

Arthur Matsu was the first Asian-American to play in the NFL. He played one season with the Dayton Triangles in 1928. He also served as an assistant coach at Rutgers.

Jim Thorpe, one of the greatest athletes in American history, was the first Native American to play in the NFL, playing from 1920–28. He also played professional baseball and was an Olympic track star. Thorpe was inducted into the Pro Football Hall of Fame in 1963.

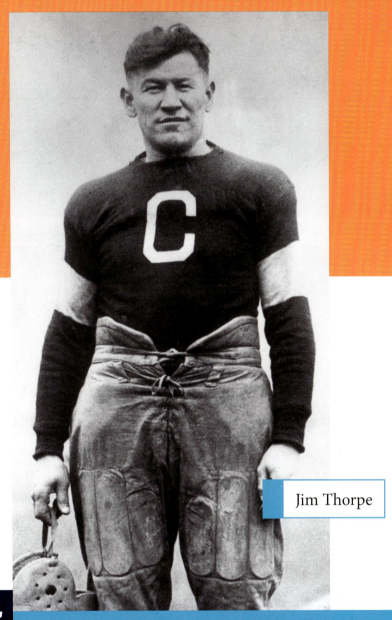

Jim Thorpe

Jim Thorpe, who played for six different NFL teams over his eight-year NFL career, won gold medals in the decathlon and pentathlon in the 1912 Olympic Games in Sweden.

Woody Strode, Jack Robinson, and Kenny Washington played for the 1939 UCLA team.

Prior to 1946, the NFL banned Black players. The first two Black players to play in the NFL were Kenny Washington and Woody Strode. Both signed contracts with the NFL in 1946.

Burl Toler became the first Black official in the NFL in 1965. He was an outstanding athlete, but he injured his knee at the end of his college career. He never played in the NFL, but he did spend 15 years as an NFL official.

While men dominate the playing field, many influential women are changing the face of football. Beth Mowins became the first woman to be lead announcer for a nationally televised NFL game in 2017. In 2015, Sarah Thomas was hired as the first full-time female official in the NFL. In 2021, she became the first woman to work a Super Bowl game.

SARAH THOMAS: TRAILBLAZER

When Sarah Thomas was in fifth grade, she wanted to play basketball, but her school didn't have a girls' team. Her aunt told her to go out for the boys' team. She did. And ever since, she's never let anything stop her. Thomas never played football, but she excelled in basketball. Her skill earned her a college scholarship.

After attending a meeting about becoming an NFL official, she pursued that career path. Within a few years, that dream came true. On September 13, 2015, Thomas made her NFL **debut** in a game between the Houston Texans and Kansas City Chiefs.

CHAPTER 4
SUPER BOWL SPECTACLES

Each of the 56 most-watched sporting events in the United States in 2023 were NFL games. Traditionally, the Super Bowl tops them all!

Travis Kelce is interviewed after winning the 2024 Super Bowl.

People who don't even care about football watch the Super Bowl. Many watch the game for the commercials. Super Bowl commercials cost a lot of money. How much? About $7 million for a 30-second commercial in 2024. Today, almost all Super Bowl commercials are new, made just for the big game. It's like a movie premiere—for commercials!

Other people watch for the halftime shows. They are mini concerts. Some of the best-reviewed halftime shows have been performances by Lady Gaga, Beyoncé, Katy Perry, and U2. But the best may have been Prince, who performed for 12 minutes in a downpour in Miami in 2007!

Prince performing at the 2007 Super Bowl

Football has come a long way. The Super Bowl is the sport's pinnacle, of course. It's the event everyone waits to see. But there would be no Super Bowl without the pioneers who created the game. What would those young men at Rutgers in 1869 say if someone had told them the new game they played would become the most popular sport in America? Or that more than 100 million people would watch the sport's biggest game? Or that the sport's best players would earn millions of dollars?

The Kansas City Chiefs line up in the shotgun formation during Super Bowl LVIII in 2024.

TIMELINE

1869 The first football game takes place between Rutgers and Princeton.

1876 Walter Camp writes the first rules of American football.

1905 Rule changes, such as the forward pass, make the game safer.

1920 The National Football League is established.

1946 The NFL ends its unofficial ban on Black players.

1960 The American Football League plays its first season.

1970 The World Professional Football Championship Trophy is renamed the Vince Lombardi Trophy.

1979 Bill Walsh brings the West Coast Offense to the San Francisco 49ers.

2009 The Women's Football Alliance is established.

2017 The New England Patriots make the biggest comeback in Super Bowl history.

2024 The Kansas City Chiefs with their third Super Bowl in five years. They joined only three other teams who have done that—the Pittsburgh Steelers, the Dallas Cowboys, and the New England Patriots

GLOSSARY

artificial turf (ar-tuh-FI-shuhl TERF)—a human-made substitute for a grass playing field

concussion (kuhn-KUH-shuhn)—an injury to the brain caused by a hard blow to the head

debut (day-BYOO)—someone's first appearance or performance

face mask (FAYSS MASK)—a protective covering for the face

interception (in-tur-SEP-shun)—a pass caught by a defensive player

racism (RAY-siz-uhm)—the belief that one race is better than other races

rusher (RUH-shur)—someone who runs with the football

sack (SAK)—when a defensive player tackles the opposing quarterback behind the line of scrimmage

scrum (SKRUM)—when players from opposing teams push together and struggle to gain possession of the ball

READ MORE

Berglund, Bruce R. *Football GOATs: The Greatest Athletes of All Time*. North Mankato, MN: Capstone Press, 2022.

Halprin, David. *Football Biographies for Kids: Stories of Football's Most Inspiring Players*. Naperville, IL: Callisto Publishing, 2024.

Smith, Elliott. *The Forgotten Four: Breaking the Color Barrier in Pro Football*. Minneapolis: Lerner Publications, 2025.

INTERNET SITES

It Started with 14 Teams in the Roaring 20's
nfl.com/100/original-towns/

National Football Foundation: Walter Camp
footballfoundation.org/hof_search.aspx?hof=2080

Pro Football Hall of Fame
profootballhof.com

INDEX

ABOUT THE AUTHOR

Robb Murray is a journalist and freelance writer who lives in Mankato, Minnesota. He earned a BS degree from Minnesota State University, Mankato. He is married and has two children and one beagle.